Friends Forever
4 Favorite Stories

Even Steven and Odd Todd
Football Friends
Hare and Rabbit: Friends Forever
Second-Grade Ape

SCHOLASTIC INC. Cartwheel ·B·O·O·K·S·®

New York   Toronto   London   Auckland   Sydney
Mexico City   New Delhi   Hong Kong   Buenos Aires

For my brother, Kevin, who's definitely a little odd
—K.C.

To Leal
—H.M.

Even Steven and Odd Todd (0-590-22715-7)
Copyright © 1996 by Scholastic Inc.

Football Friends (0-590-38395-7)
Text copyright © 1997 by Jean Marzollo.
Illustrations copyright © 1997 by True Kelley.

Hare and Rabbit: Friends Forever (0-439-08753-8)
Copyright © 2000 by Julia Noonan.

Second-Grade Ape (0-590-37261-0)
Text copyright © 1998 by Daniel Pinkwater.
Illustrations copyright © 1998 by Jill Pinkwater.

All rights reserved. Published by Scholastic Inc.
SCHOLASTIC, CARTWHEEL BOOKS, and associated logos
are trademarks and/or registered trademarks of Scholastic Inc.

ISBN 0-439-76314-2

12 11 10 9 8 7 6 5 4 3 2 1   5 6 7 8 9 10/0
Printed in the U.S.A. 56 • This compilation edition first printing, June 2005

Even Steven and Odd Todd

by **Kathryn Cristaldi**

Illustrated by **Henry B. Morehouse**

Even Steven lived on the edge of town
in a two-story house
with a four-bicycle garage.
He had six cats,
eight gerbils,
ten goldfish,
and a flower garden with twelve sprinklers.

POST OFFICE

"I'll have two loaves of bread,"
said Even Steven when he went to the bakery.
At the library he checked out four books.
At the post office he bought eight stamps.
Even Steven loved everything to be even.
"There's nothing odd about him,"
his neighbors told each other.

One day Even Steven heard a knock
on his door. He looked out the window.
It was Cousin Odd Todd.
Even Steven pulled down the shade
and turned off the lights.
"No one is home!" he shouted.

He heard three knocks.

He heard five knocks.

Then he heard seven knocks.
"Stop! Stop!" Even Steven
cried out twice.
He opened the door.

"Odd Todd," said Even Steven.
"What a surprise."
"Hey, Cuz!" came a voice from behind
three odd-shaped suitcases.
"Guess who is spending the summer with you?"

Even Steven looked up and down the street.

He looked behind the bushes.

He looked under the welcome mat.

He did not see anyone.

Except Odd Todd.

It was going to be one LONG summer.

The next morning Even Steven got up
at 8 o'clock sharp.
He was very hungry.
"I will make pancakes for breakfast," he said.
"If I make four pancakes,
I can have two now and save two for lunch.

"If I make eight pancakes,
I can have four now
and save four for lunch."
Even Steven smacked his lips.
Counting pancakes made him
very, very hungry.

He decided to make twelve pancakes.
Six for now and six for lunch.

Just then Odd Todd woke up.
It was 9 o'clock sharp.
"Yum, I smell pancakes," he said.
Odd Todd rubbed his stomach
thirteen times.

He went into the kitchen.
Even Steven was washing his plate.
He did not see his cousin.

CHOMP! CHOMP! CHOMP!

"Good morning, Cuz," said Odd Todd,
with his mouth wide open.
Even Steven's mouth fell open, too.
He stared at the plate of pancakes.
Now there were only three
odd pancakes for lunch.
"What's so good about it?"
Even Steven snapped.
He went out to work in his garden.

Even Steven loved his garden
more than anything.
"Today I will plant six rows of petunias,
eight rows..."
HONK! HONK! HONK!
Even Steven looked up.

Odd Todd rode by on a tricycle
with three wheels,
five different-colored streamers,
and a horn shaped like a parrot.
Odd Todd waved with one hand.
He was not watching where he was going.
Odd Todd rolled straight into
Even Steven's garden!

Even Steven's face turned beet-red.

Two puffs of smoke came out of his ears.

"My prize four-leaf clovers!" he shouted.

"Look what you have done!"

"I'm really, really, really sorry,"

Odd Todd said.

"I'll buy you lunch," he added.

Even Steven thought it over.

It was almost noon.

Odd Todd could not get into trouble

as long as they were together.

The pair of cousins headed for town.

Even Steven and Odd Todd
went to the pizza place.
"I would like four slices," said Even Steven.
"Two with onions and two with olives."
"I would like three slices," said Odd Todd.
"One plain, one with extra cheese,
and one with gummy worms."

Even Steven looked at his cousin's pizza.

There were nine pink worms on it.

Nine squishy, wiggly worms.

His face turned green.

"You look a little pale, Cuz," said Odd Todd.

"You should get out in the sun more."

Even Steven and Odd Todd
walked to the ice-cream shop.
"I will have two scoops of double-dip
chocolate chocolate," said Even Steven.
"I will have a triple nutty fudge sundae,"
said Odd Todd. "Extra nuts, please."
Even Steven went to look for a seat.
Odd Todd brought the ice cream.

Even Steven took a bite of his ice cream.
Then he saw something odd. It was the nuts.
There were exactly eleven.
"Nuts!" he screamed.
"Who put nuts on my double-dip
chocolate chocolate?"

Even Steven's face turned blue.

Four puffs of smoke came out of his ears.

"No need to thank me, Cuz." Odd Todd smiled.

"They were extras."

On the way home Even Steven saw a sign
in the flower shop.

Perfect Garden
Contest
BIG PRIZE

"I have a perfect garden," said Even Steven.
"It's perfect because it's perfectly even."

He wrote his name on the contest list.
"Hey, Cuz, check out this plant," said Odd Todd.
Even Steven did not answer. He ran home
and turned on his twelve sprinklers.
Then Even Steven took a nap.
He dreamed about winning the big prize.

Even Steven woke up and went
to his perfect garden.
The contest judge would be coming soon.
Even Steven counted his six rows of petunias,
his eight rows of daisies,
his ten rows of sunflowers,
and . . . one row of cactuses!
Each cactus had five long, sharp needles!
Even Steven's face turned purple.
Six puffs of smoke came out of his ears.

"That's it!" Even Steven screamed.
"I can't take you anymore, Cousin!
You are too odd!"

Just then the contest judge came over
to the garden.
"Odd, hmmm, yes. But I like it!
We have a winner!"

He handed Even Steven two tickets.

Two tickets to Twin Lakes!

Even Steven smiled.

"Now who shall I take on this trip for two?"
he asked.

"Don't worry, Cuz," Odd Todd said.

"My three bags are already packed!"

Go Philipstown Seahawks!
—J.M.

Go Warner Wildcats!
—T.K.

Football
Friends

by **Jean, Dan, and Dave Marzollo**
Illustrated by **True Kelley**

"Let's play touch football. I'll be a captain," said Freddy.

"Me, too," said Mark. "I pick Carlos."

"Why did you go first?" asked Freddy.

"Because I did," said Mark.

Freddy was mad. He wanted Carlos because Carlos had the best throwing arm.

"I pick Tommy," said Freddy.

"Sara," said Mark.

"No fair!" said Freddy. He wanted Sara on his team.

"Is too," said Mark.

"Is not," said Freddy. "I quit."

"You're a baby," said Mark.

Freddy jumped on Mark and threw him to the ground. Mark fought back. Freddy got dirt in his mouth and a bump on his head.

Suddenly a whistle blew. An aide came over. "Freddy and Mark, to the office," she said.

Freddy and Mark were mad as tigers.

"Fighting again?" asked Mrs. Smith. She was the principal.

"Freddy knocked me over," said Mark.

"Mark called me a baby," said Freddy.

Mrs. Smith looked at them. "What's the difference between a big boy and a baby?" she asked.

Freddy and Mark didn't know what to say.

"This is a baby," said Mrs. Smith. She waved her arms and made baby noises.

Mark and Freddy began to laugh.

Mrs. Smith laughed, too. "I'm glad we got that straight. Now tell me. What were you two really fighting about?"

"We were going to play football," said Freddy. "Mark and I were captains. But it wasn't fair. He had the better team. So I quit. That's when he called me a baby."

"And that's when you lost your temper," said Mrs. Smith. She looked worried. "Is football too rough for you to play?"

"No!" said both boys. "We use a foam ball, and we just play touch. No one tackles. No one gets hurt."

Mrs. Smith smiled. "I'm glad that you two agree on something. And usually you are friends, right?"

"Right," said Freddy and Mark.

"Then why do you always fight when you play this game?" she asked.

Freddy pointed to Mark. "He always gets the better team."

"*He* always loses his temper," said Mark.

"That's because the teams are uneven," said Freddy.

"I have an idea," said Mrs. Smith. "I'm going to give you football homework. I want you to work on it together. Your job is to make two even teams."

That night Freddy and Mark talked on the phone. Their homework was hard, but they did it.

The next day they gave their lists to Mrs. Smith.

Recess came. Kids met on the playground to play touch football. Mrs. Smith came, too. She showed the kids the chart.

"Are these teams fair?" she asked.

"Yes," said the kids.

"Fine," said Mrs. Smith. "Then you may play touch football. But you must use these teams. And if there is any more fighting, there will be no more football. Do you understand?"

Everyone said yes.

The teams got set. Mark and Freddy were opposite each other. The game began.

Freddy hiked the ball to Tommy. Tommy flipped it to Sara. The ball bounced off her hands. It flew into the air.

Freddy caught it before it hit the ground.

He ran all the way to the pavement and scored!

The Cowboys were ahead 7–0. Each touchdown was worth seven points. There were no extra points in their playground game.

The Raiders now had the ball. Mark hiked the ball to Carlos. Carlos ran to the left. He saw Mark on the other side of the field. Carlos threw a pass to Mark.

Mark caught it and ran toward the end zone.

Freddy ran as fast as he could after him. He wished he could run faster. He didn't want Mark to score.

Freddy finally caught up with Mark. Freddy reached out to touch him. There! He touched him!

But Mark kept running. He crossed the goal line.

"Touchdown!" Mark shouted.

"No way!" cried Freddy. "I touched you!"

"You did not!" yelled Mark. "I didn't feel a thing!"

Freddy ran at Mark and started to push him.

"Cut it out, Freddy!" said Sara. "Mrs. Smith is watching. Don't you remember what she said? If there's fighting, no more football."

Freddy let up. But he was still mad.

The score was now 7–7, and recess was almost over.

Freddy wanted to win!

The Cowboys and the Raiders lined up.
Freddy and Mark were face-to-face.

"You're going to lose," said Mark,
"because you're a baby. I can say whatever I
want because now you can't fight me."

Freddy gave Mark a shove.

"Time out!" said Tommy. "Huddle up, team!"

The Cowboys formed a circle.

"Freddy, keep your cool!" hissed Sara.

"He called me a baby," said Freddy. "What am I supposed to do? Say thank you?"

Sara was disgusted. "He's just trying to get you mad so you won't play well."

"Don't pay any attention to Mark," said Tommy. "Use your anger to run faster. Okay?"

The teams lined up.

"Baby," said Mark. "Ga-ga. Goo-goo!"

This really made Freddy mad. But instead of hitting Mark, he thought about Sara's words: *He's just trying to get you mad so you won't play well.* Her words made sense.

Then he remembered what Tommy had said. *Use your anger to run faster.*

"Ga-ga. Goo-goo!" said Mark again.

Freddy pretended he didn't hear. But inside his rage burned. Freddy pretended it was like rocket fuel! He hiked the ball back to Tommy and ran toward the goal. He turned his head to look back.

Tommy aimed and fired. The ball was coming right to Freddy!

Freddy reached up for it.

Freddy caught the ball and brought it down to his chest. Then he ran as fast as he could. He heard footsteps behind him. But Freddy was too fast for anyone to catch. He blasted into the end zone.

"Ga-ga. Goo-goo!" Freddy shouted as he crossed the line.

"Ga-ga. Goo-goo!" sang Sara and Tommy. The Cowboys waved their arms and toddled like babies.

It was the first football game they had won in a long time. It was also the first game without a big fight.

Later, Mrs. Smith stopped Freddy in the hall. "I want to talk with you," she said. "I wasn't fighting!" said Freddy.

Mrs. Smith smiled. "I don't only talk to kids when they've done something wrong. Sometimes I talk to them when they have done something right. I heard Mark tease you, and I saw what you did. You almost lost your cool. But then you controlled your temper."

Freddy blushed. "My team helped me," he said.

"That's the way to handle teasers," she said. "If you ignore them, they'll give up teasing you. That's one way to stay out of fights."

Freddy smiled.

"I don't think I'll mind if Mark teases me again," he said. "Thanks to him, I scored a touchdown."

For Wendy, the saver of everything.
Marie, the mind reader.
Tina, my first 4-ever friend.
—J.N.

with love and thanks to
Barbara Seuling
&

Ellen Dreyer	*Catherine Nichols*
Constance Foland	*Roxane Orgill*
Marthe Jocelyn	*Michele Spirn*
Agnes Martinez	*Roseann Yaman*

Hare and Rabbit

FRIENDS FOREVER

by **Julia Noonan**

Hare ⟋Rabbit
Cleaning House

Hare and Rabbit lived together
in a little house in the woods.

One day, Rabbit picked up an old pair
of garden boots.
"Our house is too messy," she told Hare.
"There is no room for us. We must throw
things away."
"But, Rabbit," said Hare. "We do not know
what things we might need later on."

"We do not need these old newspapers,"
said Rabbit. "And we do not need boots
with holes in them, either."
Rabbit threw them all out the door.

"You're right," said Hare.
She began gathering things to throw
away, too.
"Good-bye, empty shoe box.
Good-bye, dried-up, old paintbrush.
Good-bye, old book with torn pages.
I will miss you!"

Soon a giant pile grew outside the door.
Rabbit threw away a little table
that wiggled.
Then Rabbit looked at the chairs
by the fireplace.
"They are old," she said, pointing
to them.

The inside of the house got emptier
and emptier.
"Look!" said Rabbit. "Our house has
so much room, I can do cartwheels."

"See how pretty our rug is," said Hare.
"We have not seen it in a long time."
Hare and Rabbit sat on their pretty rug.
"Now what?" asked Hare.
"Now we enjoy our clean house,"
said Rabbit. "We can have tea."

"Good idea," said Hare.
She went to the kitchen.
But she could not find the pot
to make tea.
"Where is the teapot?" asked Hare.
"The teapot had a big chip in it, so
I threw it away," said Rabbit.
"Use a pan instead."
Hare made the tea. She carried it in
on a tray.
"Where should I put it?" asked Hare.
"Set it on the floor, I guess," said Rabbit.

"I miss the little table that wiggled,"
said Hare.
"Where is my cup?" asked Rabbit.
"It had a chip in it, too," said Hare.
She poured the tea.
"It does not feel right having tea on
the floor without my cup," said Rabbit.
"And I miss my chair."
"I miss a lot of things," said Hare.
Hare looked at Rabbit.
Rabbit looked at Hare.
Together, they went outside.

It was dark when they were done
putting everything back in its place.
Hare put the tray on the little table
that wiggled. Then she poured the tea.
"It feels so cozy having all of our things
around us again," she said.

"You are so right," said Rabbit.
"If we want to do cartwheels,
we can always do them outside." ❖

Hare and Rabbit
Mind-Reader Ring

One morning Hare sat down
to breakfast.
Rabbit was already at the table.
"Where is the prize from the new
box of cereal?" asked Hare, peeking
into the box.

"I already have it," said Rabbit.
"What is it?" asked Hare.
"It is a magic mind-reader ring,"
said Rabbit. "Now I know everything
you are thinking."

"Can you tell me what I am
thinking right now?" asked Hare.
"Yes," said Rabbit. "You're thinking
that you wish you got the ring."
"You're right," said Hare.

Hare walked out of the kitchen
into the living room.
She called back to Rabbit.
"Can you tell me what I am thinking now?"
"Yes," said Rabbit. "You're wondering
if I can read your mind when you are in
a different room."

"Oh, dear!" said Hare, as she walked back into the kitchen. "You *do* know what I'm thinking."
"Of course," said Rabbit. "Now think of something else."
Hare thought, *I do not like Rabbit reading my mind.*

Rabbit said, "You're thinking about
which kind of cereal to eat. Am I right?"
Hare felt much better.
"Right again!" said Hare.
"Really?" asked Rabbit.
"Really," said Hare.

Hare smiled as she put cereal in her bowl.
Hare thought, *I love Carrot Crunch
cereal.* "And what am I thinking now?"
asked Hare.
"You're trying to decide if you want juice
or tea," said Rabbit.

"Oh, Rabbit. You're so clever," said Hare. "Perhaps we should hang out a sign that says, 'Mind-Reader Rabbit the Great lives here.'"

"Do you think that is a good idea?" asked Rabbit.
"Yes," said Hare. "And I will be your helper, in a beautiful costume. I can't wait. I'm going to make the sign right now. It will tell the *whole world* you can read minds."

"The *whole world*?" said Rabbit.
"Yes," said Hare. "Everyone will come.
You will read all of their minds."
"Wait a minute," said Rabbit.
"The ring feels very strange. I think it
may be losing its power."
"Give me the ring," said Hare.

Rabbit gave Hare the ring.
Hare tried it on. "You're right," she said,
taking it off again.
"The ring has lost its power. But I bet
I know what you are thinking anyway."
"What?" asked Rabbit.
"That it's time to eat," said Hare. ❖

Hare and Rabbit

Boo-Boo Bunny

"Look!" said Rabbit. "A letter has come
from my old friend Boo-Boo."

Hare's long ears stood straight up.
"You never told me you had a friend
named Boo-Boo."
"I knew her a long time ago," said Rabbit.
"We used to work together at the circus."

Rabbit opened the envelope
and read the card inside.
"Great news!" she said. "Boo-Boo
is riding bareback in a circus that
is coming to our town."
Rabbit held up two tickets.
"We're invited to join her
under the Big Top."

Rabbit handed Hare the card.
One side had a picture and said:

> *Boo-Boo Bunny*
> *Bareback Ballerina!*

"She looks like a very fancy bunny,"
said Hare.
Hare turned the card over.
The other side said:

> *See you at the circus!*
> *Love, Boo-Boo*

Hare thought to herself: *Boo-Boo . . .*
what a silly name.
"We better hurry," said Rabbit suddenly.
"The circus is today!"

The stands were full when Hare
and Rabbit got to the circus.
The clowns were doing silly tricks.

Then out came the horses into the ring.
With them came a beautiful bunny.
She wore fancy, sparkling clothes.
She had feathers in her hair
and satin slippers on her feet.
"It's Boo-Boo!" said Rabbit.

Everyone cheered as Boo-Boo
did her tricks.
She jumped from horse to horse,
and off and on again.
"That doesn't look so very hard to do,"
said Hare quietly.
"Look at her," said Rabbit. "She is the
best bareback rider anywhere!"
"She looks like a show-off to me,"
said Hare.

When the circus was over, Rabbit said
to Hare, "Did you like the show?"
"Yes, I did," said Hare. "But I would not
call a bunny who jumps on horses
a ballerina."
Hare and Rabbit walked toward
Boo-Boo's circus wagon.

"That tail of hers," said Hare.
"It was too fluffy to be her *real* tail."
"Is something wrong?" asked Rabbit.
"You have not even met Boo-Boo yet,
but you act as if you don't like her."
Hare and Rabbit walked a little ways
in silence.

At last, Hare said, "I don't like her
because you like her *so much*.
I'm afraid you like her better than me."
Rabbit gave Hare a big hug.
"No one could ever take
your place, Hare," she said.

When they reached the wagon,
Boo-Boo was waiting.
She did not look so fancy now
without her costume.

After Boo-Boo and Rabbit hugged hello,
Rabbit smiled at Hare.
"Boo-Boo," said Rabbit, "I want you
to meet my very best friend." ❖

To Bushman —
With apologies for last time

Second-Grade
APE

by **Daniel Pinkwater**
Illustrated by **Jill Pinkwater**

CHAPTER 1

A VERY BIG CAT

Flash Fleetwood was walking in the woods behind his house, when he found an animal. It was quite a big animal. It was bigger than Flash Fleetwood. Flash Fleetwood was just walking along, and there it was, sitting under a bush, eating a leaf.

Flash Fleetwood watched the animal for a while. It sat quietly and watched him. It didn't seem to be afraid.

"What kind of animal is this?" Flash Fleetwood asked himself.

Maybe it is a cat, he thought. "Are you a cat?" he asked the animal.

"Whoop! Whoop! Whoop whoop whoop!" said the animal.

Flash Fleetwood had a chocolate chip cookie
in his pocket.

"Here, cat. Do you want this cookie?" he
asked. He held the cookie out to the animal.

The animal took the cookie and ate it slowly.
He looked at Flash Fleetwood with eyes full
of love.

I will take this cat home, Flash Fleetwood thought.

"Cat, do you want to come home with me?" he asked the animal.

"Whoop! Whoop!" the animal said.

"I think that means yes. Come on, cat."

Flash Fleetwood walked home through the woods. The animal followed him, tearing off branches as it went and whooping from time to time. Sometimes it would leap into the trees and swing from branch to branch.

Unusual cat, Flash Fleetwood thought.

Flash Fleetwood arrived at his house.

His father was outside. He was punishing the chickens.

"You chickens will stand facing the corner," Flash Fleetwood's father said, "until you learn it is wrong to make fun of humans."

"Hello, Freddie," his father said. "What have you been up to?"

Flash Fleetwood's real name was Freddie. His father never called him Flash. He always called him Freddie.

"Hello, Dad. See the big cat I found."

"That is no cat, Freddie. That is a gorilla," Flash Fleetwood's father said.

"Really?" Flash Fleetwood asked.

"I am sure of it," his father said.

"Will you let me keep him?" Flash Fleetwood asked.

"He might be a lost gorilla, Freddie," Flash Fleetwood's father said. "His owners might be looking for him. We will look in the newspaper and telephone the animal shelter. If no one is advertising for a lost gorilla, maybe — just maybe — you may keep him."

Then he called to Flash Fleetwood's mother, "Mother! Come and see Freddie's gorilla!"

Flash Fleetwood's mother came out of the kitchen door. She was mixing up a big bowl of lunch. She held the bowl in her arm, and mixed the lunch with a wooden spoon.

"My goodness! It really is a gorilla!" Flash Fleetwood's mother said.

"He thought it was a cat," Flash Fleetwood's father said.

"That boy!" Flash Fleetwood's mother said. "What will he bring home next? It is quite a nice gorilla, isn't it?"

Then she said, "Shall we let him keep it?"

"Why not?" Flash Fleetwood's father said. "If no one advertises for a lost gorilla for a week, and if no one has come looking for one at the animal shelter, we might let him keep it, don't you think?"

"It is quite a nice gorilla," Flash Fleetwood's mother said again. "We'll have to see. But now, come to lunch. It's egg salad pie and raw spinach. Do you think the gorilla will like that?"

The gorilla ate all the raw spinach.

"You thought he was a cat?" Flash Fleetwood's mother asked.

"Only at first," Flash Fleetwood said.

"He is much bigger than a cat," Flash Fleetwood's father said.

"It was dark where I found him," Flash Fleetwood said.

"He is twenty times bigger than a cat," Flash Fleetwood's mother said.

"Look, I made a mistake, OK?" Flash Fleetwood said.

"It is funny that you thought it was a cat," Flash Fleetwood's father said.

"Anybody can make a mistake," Flash Fleetwood said.

"Of course, dear," Flash Fleetwood's mother said.

"You were lucky to find a gorilla," his father said.

"May I show the gorilla to Bullets Birkenstock?" Flash Fleetwood asked his parents.

"He should have a bath first," Flash Fleetwood's mother said.

"Please. We'll come back soon," Flash Fleetwood said.

"Come back soon and give the gorilla a bath,"
Flash Fleetwood's mother said.

"I will," said Flash Fleetwood.

CHAPTER 2

BULLETS BIRKENSTOCK

Bullets Birkenstock was Flash Fleetwood's best friend. Bullets Birkenstock's real name was Bruce Birkenstock.

They made up their nicknames themselves.

Nobody but Bullets Birkenstock called Freddie Fleetwood "Flash" Fleetwood. Nobody else called him that.

Only Flash Fleetwood called Bruce Birkenstock "Bullets" Birkenstock. Nobody else called him that.

Bullets Birkenstock was smart. He was the smartest person Flash Fleetwood knew. He knew a lot about animals.

Bullets Birkenstock had a dog named Rolf. Bullets Birkenstock was teaching Rolf to talk. Already Rolf could say his name.

"What's your name?" Bullets Birkenstock would say.

"Rolf! Rolf!" Rolf would bark.

"See?" Bullets Birkenstock would say. "He said 'Rolf.' He can say his name."

Flash Fleetwood walked to Bullets Birkenstock's house. He led the gorilla by holding one of its fingers. Its fingers were the size of bananas. The gorilla walked behind Flash Fleetwood and shuffled its feet along the sidewalk.

"You are a nice, tame gorilla," Flash Fleetwood said.

The gorilla whooped to Flash Fleetwood.

They came to Bullets Birkenstock's house.
Flash Fleetwood knocked on the door.

"Bullets Birkenstock, come out and see what
I have!" Flash Fleetwood called.

Bullets Birkenstock came out.

"Leaping lollipops!" Bullets Birkenstock said.
"Look at the size of that cat!"

"Leaping lollipops!" was something Bullets
Birkenstock liked to say.

"Ha!" Flash Fleetwood said. "It is not a cat."

"It is not a cat? What is it?" Bullets Birkenstock asked.

"It is a gorilla," Flash Fleetwood said.

"Leaping lollipops!" Bullets Birkenstock said.

"Ha! You thought it was a cat," Flash Fleetwood said.

"Only at first," Bullets Birkenstock said. "You were standing in the shadows with it. It is a neat gorilla. I can see that now."

"Whoop! Whoop! Whoop whoop whoop!"
the gorilla said.

"Are they going to let you keep him?" Bullets
Birkenstock asked.

"Why not?" Flash Fleetwood said. "If nobody
advertises in the paper for a week, and if nobody
asks for him at the animal shelter, he is mine.
My gorilla. Finders keepers."

"Wow! Lucky! What is his name?" Bullets Birkenstock asked.

"His name is Phil," Flash Fleetwood said.

"Phil?" Bullets Birkenstock asked.

"Phil the gorilla," Flash Fleetwood said. "I made up my mind on the way over here."

"Let's have Phil meet Rolf," Bullets Birkenstock said.

Bullets Birkenstock called his dog.

Rolf saw Phil.

Phil saw Rolf.

"Whoop! Whoop! Whoop whoop whoop!"
said Phil.

"Yipe!" said Rolf.

Rolf was afraid of Phil. He cringed. He
cowered. He put his tail between his legs. He
looked as though he wanted to run away, but
wasn't sure what the gorilla would do if he did.

"Look, Rolf. He's a good gorilla," Bullets Birkenstock said.

Flash Fleetwood and Bullets Birkenstock patted Phil.

"See? Don't be scared of him," they said.

Phil said "Whoop!" very softly.

Rolf wagged his tail.

It was a very small wag.

Phil patted Rolf.

Rolf wagged his tail a little more. He still wasn't sure, but he wasn't quite so scared.

"Let's all go for a walk," Flash Fleetwood said.

"Let's walk in the woods," Bullets Birkenstock said.

"Woof," Rolf said.

"Whoop!" Phil said.

CHAPTER 3

IN THE WOODS

In the woods, Phil showed off his tricks.

He could climb very high. He could swing from tree to tree. He could fall, crashing through branches. And he could fall on his head. He never got hurt.

Phil could pick up big logs. He could run through the woods. He could whoop very loudly. He could pound on his chest. It sounded like a drum. He could eat leaves. He could pick up things with his feet.

Flash Fleetwood, Bullets Birkenstock, and Rolf were filled with admiration.

"He is the greatest gorilla who ever lived," Bullets Birkenstock said.

"Yes, he is," Flash Fleetwood said.

"Do you think, if you are ever sick, or have to go away, or if you die, Phil could stay at my house?" Bullets Birkenstock asked.

"If I am sick, or if I have to go away, or if I die, Phil can stay with you," Flash Fleetwood said. "You are my best friend."

"Could he stay at my house, just for one night, even if you don't die or anything?" Bullets Birkenstock asked.

"Maybe later," Flash Fleetwood said. "After he has settled down and gotten used to me. Maybe then."

"Wow," Bullets Birkenstock said.

Bullets Birkenstock had brought cookies.

The boys and the dog and the gorilla sat on a log. They each ate a cookie.

"You know, Phil is a neat animal," Bullets Birkenstock said.

"He sure is," Flash Fleetwood said. "I'm going to bring him to school tomorrow."

"Leaping lollipops!" said Bullets Birkenstock.

CHAPTER 4

BREAKFAST WITH A GORILLA

Flash Fleetwood asked his parents, "May I take my gorilla to school tomorrow?"

"Only if you give him a bath," Flash Fleetwood's mother said.

Giving a bath to a gorilla is a big project. It took more than an hour, and the bathroom got very wet. Flash Fleetwood had to clean the bathroom, too. And it took all the towels to get Phil dry.

"If you are going to have a pet, you have to take care of it," Flash Fleetwood's mother said.

"Where will Phil sleep?" Flash Fleetwood asked.

Flash Fleetwood's father had found a book about gorillas.

"Gorillas like to make nests to sleep in," Flash Fleetwood's father told him. "Sometimes a nest in a tree, and sometimes a nest on the ground. They like to feel protected."

Flash Fleetwood helped Phil make a nest of blankets in his closet. Phil liked it. He curled up and went to sleep.

In the morning, Phil was not in his nest. Flash Fleetwood ran downstairs. Phil was in the kitchen with his mother and father. They were eating pancakes. Flash Fleetwood ate some, too. Flash Fleetwood's mother ate some. Flash Fleetwood's father ate a lot of pancakes. Phil the gorilla ate a great many pancakes. He ate more than twenty pancakes. He used all the maple syrup. He drank six glasses of milk. He ate five bananas, which were all the bananas in the house. He ate two apples. He ate an orange.

"Phil has a good appetite," Flash Fleetwood's father said.

"It will be expensive, shopping for a gorilla," Flash Fleetwood's mother said.

"Oh, pancakes don't cost very much," Flash Fleetwood's father said.

CHAPTER 5

SECOND-GRADE APE

Flash Fleetwood and Phil got to school early. Flash Fleetwood left Phil in the hall and went into his classroom.

His teacher was Mrs. Hotdogbun. She always came to school early.

"Mrs. Hotdogbun, I brought my pet to school," Flash Fleetwood said.

"We do not bring pets to school, Freddie," Mrs. Hotdogbun said.

"It is an unusual pet," Flash Fleetwood said. "I thought I would show it to the class."

"Oh. Unusual pets are different," Mrs. Hotdogbun said. "But you should have asked first."

"I asked my mother. She said it would be all right," Flash Fleetwood said.

"Well, in that case, I am sure it will be all right," Mrs. Hotdogbun said. "Is it a mouse? Some children have mice as pets."

"No, it is not a mouse," Flash Fleetwood said.

"Is it a lizard?" Mrs. Hotdogbun asked. "I like lizards very much."

"No, it is not a lizard," Flash Fleetwood said.

"Is it a fish?" Mrs. Hotdogbun asked. "Fish make very nice pets."

"No," said Flash Fleetwood. "It is not a fish."

"What sort of pet is it?" Mrs. Hotdogbun asked.

"My pet is in the hall," Flash Fleetwood said. "I will bring it in."

Flash Fleetwood went out to the hall.
Phil was looking at the drawings on the walls.
He brought Phil into the classroom.
"This is Phil," Flash Fleetwood said.
"Eeek!" Mrs. Hotdogbun said.
"Whoop!" Phil said.
"That is a GORILLA!"
"Yes!" said Flash Fleetwood. "Bullets
Birkenstock thought it was a cat."
"Whoop!" said Phil.

"Freddie, is this a tame gorilla? Is he gentle?"

"He is tame. He is gentle," Flash Fleetwood said.

"I hope so," said Mrs. Hotdogbun. "I sincerely hope so."

"Phil is the finest gorilla who ever lived," Flash Fleetwood said.

"Your gorilla must sit in my own personal closet," Mrs. Hotdogbun said. "He must sit there and be very quiet. Can he do that?"

"Yes," said Flash Fleetwood. "He sat in my closet all night. He was very quiet."

"Has the gorilla had a bath?" Mrs. Hotdogbun asked.

"Yes," said Flash Fleetwood. "He had a bath last night."

"Good," said Mrs. Hotdogbun. "I will tell you when it is time to show him to the children."

Flash Fleetwood took Phil to the closet.
"Now sit here, and be very quiet," Flash
Fleetwood said.
"Whoop," said Phil quietly.

The children came in and took their seats. Bullets Birkenstock was with them.

"Where's Phil?" Bullets Birkenstock asked Flash Fleetwood.

"Wait," Flash Fleetwood said.

"Class," Mrs. Hotdogbun said, "Freddie has brought his unusual pet to show us."

"Not another mouse!" someone shouted.

"Is it a lizard?" someone else shouted. "I hate lizards."

"It had better not be a boring fish, Freddie!" someone else shouted.

"Hush!" Mrs. Hotdogbun said. "Freddie, you may go to my closet and get your pet."

Freddie went to Mrs. Hotdogbun's closet.

He took Phil by the finger and led him out.

"Yaaaaaay!" the children shouted.

"This is my pet," Flash Fleetwood said.

"Yaaaaaay!"

"His name is Phil."

"Yaaaaaay!"

"He is a gorilla."

"Yaaaaaay!"

"Mrs. Hotdogbun, if we take Phil outside he can do some tricks on the jungle gym," Flash Fleetwood said.

"We will put our coats on now," Mrs. Hotdogbun said. "We will go outside and watch Phil. We will go quietly through the halls."

"Yaaaaaay!" the children shouted quietly.

Outside, Phil did some tricks on the jungle gym.

After doing his tricks, Phil came back to the classroom.

He sat in the back of the room. He sat there for the rest of the day. Mrs. Hotdogbun gave Phil some paints. He painted some pictures.

She gave him an orange. He ate the orange. He was very quiet. He was no trouble at all.

At the end of the day, Mrs. Hotdogbun said, "Phil is a very good gorilla. He is quiet. He is no trouble at all."

"Could Phil come back tomorrow?" some children asked. "Could Phil come to school every day?"

"Yes!" the children shouted. "Let Phil come to school every day."

"Let Phil be in our class!"

"But, children, Phil is a gorilla," Mrs. Hotdogbun said.

"He is a very good gorilla!"
"He is no trouble at all."
"You said so yourself!"
"Please, Mrs. Hotdogbun! Let Phil come
to school every day!" the children shouted.
"Let him be in our class!"
"Please?"
"Well," Mrs. Hotdogbun said. "Why not?"